TESSIE
Tames Her Tongue

A Book About Learning When to Talk and When to Listen

Melissa Martin

Illustrated by
Charles Lehman

free spirit
PUBLISHING®

Text copyright © 2017 by Melissa Martin
Illustrations copyright © 2017 by Free Spirit Publishing Inc.

Library of Congress Cataloging-in-Publication Data
Names: Martin, Melissa, 1959– author. | Lehman, Charles L., illustrator.
Title: Tessie tames her tongue : a book about learning when to talk and when to listen / Melissa Martin ; illustrated by Charles Lehman.
Description: Minneapolis : Free Spirit Publishing, 2017. | Audience: Age: 5–9. |
Identifiers: LCCN 2017007581 (print) | LCCN 2017024457 (ebook) | ISBN 9781631981890 (Web PDF) | ISBN 9781631981906 (ePub) |
    ISBN 9781631981333 (hardback) | ISBN 1631981331 (hardcover)
Subjects: LCSH: Listening—Juvenile literature. | Etiquette for children and teenagers. | BISAC: JUVENILE FICTION / Social Issues / Manners
    & Etiquette.
Classification: LCC BF323.L5 (ebook) | LCC BF323.L5 M357 2017 (print) | DDC 177/.2—dc23
LC record available at https://lccn.loc.gov/2017007581

Reading Level Grade 2; Interest Level Ages 5–9
Fountas & Pinnell Guided Reading Level M

Cover and interior design by Emily Dyer
Edited by Brian Farrey-Latz

10 9 8 7 6 5 4 3 2 1
Printed in China
R18860517

Free Spirit Publishing Inc.
6325 Sandburg Road, Suite 100
Minneapolis, MN 55427-3674
(612) 338-2068
help4kids@freespirit.com
www.freespirit.com

Free Spirit offers competitive pricing.
Contact edsales@freespirit.com for pricing information on multiple quantity purchases.

Dedication
To my daughter, Amber—
my heart and hope.

Acknowledgments
Appreciation and gratitude to
Brian, an awesome editor, and all
the folks at Free Spirit Publishing.

Tessie is a talker. Morning, noon, and night.
Phew! That's a lot of talking.

I visited a butterfly house at an observatory yesterday. Wow! I saw a monarch, a tiger swallowtail, a red admiral, an American snout, a Goliath birdwing. . .

When her family watches a movie, Tessie talks and talks.

POPCORN. Is it corn that pops? I think it should be called Cornpops.

"Shhhhhh," says her brother.
"We're trying to watch the movie.
You're such a blabby gabby."

ERGGGH! But I need to tell you that **popcorn kernels** can **pop** up to three feet in the air. I read that fact **in a book.**

"Shhhish," says her father. "Let's have some quiet."

Tessie, the fast talker, talks when she eats ice cream.

Dad, is there such a thing as hotdog-flavored ice cream? I'd like to try it. But I wouldn't put mustard and onions on it. Maybe I'll invent pizza-flavored ice cream.

Whaaaaoohh! Owie! Yowie! Brain freeze! Is there a scientific name for an ice cream headache?

"Gross!" hollers her brother. "Don't talk with your mouth full!" But Tessie doesn't hear him.

Every day, Tessie talks on the school bus the whole way to school. She talks to the bus driver . . .

. . . to the kids beside her . . .

I need to make a **What** should I do? out of clay. **Red coloring,** baking bubbled out **and** It didn't really but it was

. . . in front of her . . .

. . . in back of her . . .

science project. I once made a volcano lava made of food soda, and vinegar down the sides. explode messy.

. . . and across the aisle from her.

At school, Tessie talks as she takes her seat in the classroom.

Guess what? I visited a planetarium and took a field trip through the solar system without leaving the earth! And online, I learned about geology. Did you know that rocks tell a tale by their fossils? Igneous, sedimentary, and metamorphic are the three types of rocks.

"Hello, class. Let's start today with show and tell," says Mrs. Hardy, the teacher. "Who has something to share?"

I saw the **cutest meerkats** on TV! They communicate with **sounds** like we do. They **purr** when they're **happy** and **chatter** when they're **scared**.

Tessie doesn't hear Mrs. Hardy. She keeps yapping and yakking.

"Everyone, remember to raise your hand before speaking," Mrs. Hardy says. "That's the rule in our classroom. It helps everyone listen while one person talks."

Tessie raises her hand high into the air.

She waves her arm several times.

My hand is raised! Look at my hand! Look at my hand!

"Class, to make sure that everyone has a chance to be heard, we're going to start using a talking stick. We'll take turns passing it around and you may only talk when you have the stick. When you don't have the stick, it's your job to listen carefully to the person talking."

Mrs. Hardy says, "Everyone will take turns talking. You need to wait your turn, Tessie."

Can I please have the talking stick? I want to talk.

TALKING STICK

During recess, Tessie talks and talks and talks. She tells the girls about her heroes.

When the girls run away to swing, she jabbers at the boys.

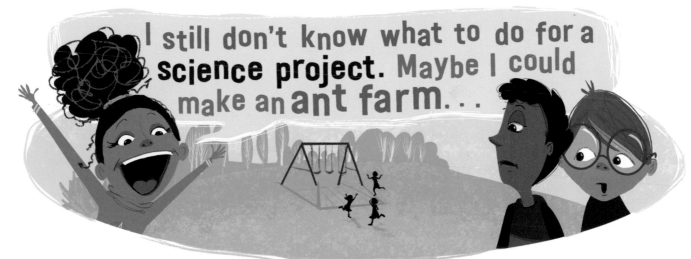

When the boys run away to play soccer, Tessie finds herself all alone. *Why did everyone go away?* she thinks.

After recess, Tessie goes to talk to Mrs. Hardy.

"I don't know what to do," Tessie says softly. "My family tells me to shush, my classmates run away. It makes me sad. Why doesn't anyone want to listen to me?"

"Tessie, you have some fascinating stories to tell, but you need to learn to listen to others as well," says Mrs. Hardy. "I know someone who can help you lasso that tongue and open those ears."

"Huh," says Tessie. "You mean I have to tame my tongue?" She imagines herself trying to lasso her tongue, as if it were a wild stallion.

Together, Mrs. Hardy and Tessie visit Mr. Abel, the school counselor, in his office.

Mr. Abel asks, "What's the problem, Tessie?"

"Can you help me, Mr. Abel? I need to tame my tongue. I like to talk about all the things that are in my head. But sometimes . . . well, maybe I talk too much."

Mr. Abel nods. "I might be able to help. Let's think about this: What do you think a good listener does?"

Tessie imagines the times when other people listened to her. "I think a good listener pays attention. A good listener looks at the person talking and stays quiet."

"Very true!" says Mr. Abel. "Good listeners also keep their mouths closed and relax their tongues."

"That sounds so hard!" Tessie says.

"Yes, sometimes, it can be hard. But you know what? You've been a good listener for me while I've been talking. That shows you can do it."

This makes Tessie feel better. She *could* be a good listener! "But what do I do when my tongue wants to speed off on its own?"

"When your tongue wants to speed off, that's a sign you need to slow down. Sometimes, when I want to slow down, I take three deep belly breaths. Do some with me."

Together, Tessie and Mr. Abel practice taking three deep breaths—slowly in through their noses and slowly out through their mouths.

"What else could you do to keep your tongue quiet?" Mr. Abel asks.

"I could curl my toes ten times," she says. "That would slow me down."

"Excellent!" Mr. Abel hands Tessie a marker. "You make a plan for taming your tongue and I'll help."

Focus on what the person talking is saying. When the person is done talking, ask him or her questions.

Imagine squeezing a lemon. Squeeze, then let go. Imagine smelling a beautiful flower.

Tessie writes:

To be a good listener, I will:
Keep my eyes on the person
talking, close my mouth, and
relax my tongue.

To stop my tongue from
speeding away, I will: Take
three deep belly breaths
and curl my toes ten times.

"This looks like a good plan," Mr. Abel says. "Remember, this will take practice. Come back and see me every Friday and we'll see how you're doing."

Tessie can feel her tongue start to dance and prance in her mouth so she takes three deep belly breaths. Air goes into her nose slowly and out through her mouth.

"Ahhhhhh." She imagines sniffing a red and white peppermint flower and blowing the petals. Her mouth stays quiet.

Tessie tells her parents about the plan to tame her talkative tongue.

"I'm going to be a tongue tamer."

"I know you can do it," says her mother.

"I know you can do it," says her father.

"I doubt it," says her brother.

MY PLAN TO TAME
MY TONGUE!

For the next few weeks, everywhere she goes, Tessie practices the skills that Mr. Abel taught her. At first, it's very hard. She still wants to gab. But Tessie does her best and, day by day, she becomes a better listener.

When others talk, she looks into their eyes and pays attention to their words. She waits until they're finished talking, then asks questions about what the speaker was talking about.

When it comes time to present her science project, no one is surprised when Tessie does a report on the tongue. She tells her class fun facts about the tongue. "Do you know your tongue has eight muscles and 3,000 to 10,000 taste buds? Tongues are about four inches long and girls have shorter tongues than boys. And sticking out your tongue at people in North America is rude, but it's a greeting in Tibet."

When Tessie goes to see Mr. Abel for their weekly Friday meeting, he says, "Congratulations! Because you've made progress, you no longer need to visit me every week. Keep practicing these skills. I'm very proud of you for learning how to tame your tongue."

"Me, too! Thanks for helping me!" says Tessie.

A few days later, Mrs. Hardy talks to Tessie's parents. "Tessie is listening more and talking less in the classroom. Her schoolwork is excellent. She is a leader and helps in the classroom. She likes fun facts and tells funny stories that make everyone laugh. I'm proud of her."

"We're proud of her, too," says Tessie's father.

"We give her 15 minutes of Tessie-Talk-Time during dinner and she no longer talks with her mouth full," says her mother.

Tessie imagines taming her tongue and doesn't interrupt.

The next week, a new boy named Tommy joins Mrs. Hardy's class. He talks without the talking stick.

He talks at lunch with his mouth full. He talks so much that the other kids run away from him at recess. Tessie knows how he feels.

"Why does everyone run away?" Tommy asks. "Why doesn't anybody listen to me?"

Tessie grins. "You know what? I might be able to help . . ."

Tips for Helping Talkative Children

The art of self-expression is learned. Children with lots to say are curious about the world and want to share their new knowledge and discoveries. It's important to encourage this side of a child's growth and development but it's equally vital to temper it with an understanding that communication isn't one sided. To effectively communicate, everyone must learn to balance talking with effective listening and thinking.

Helping talkative children learn and practice communication skills is beneficial at home, at school, and in the community. When working with a talkative child, try the following techniques.

The TLT Triangle: Thinking, Listening, Talking

The Thinking, Listening, Talking (TLT) Triangle is a helpful visual tool that can show children the key factors of communication. All three factors work together so individuals can share thoughts, feelings, opinions, and ideas. Knowing how to balance thinking, listening, talking is an important part of relationship-building and the ability to understand socialization skills.

Re-create the TLT Triangle diagram (found at right) or download a template at freespirit.com, and ask the child to draw a brain next to *thinking*, ears next to *listening*, and a mouth or lips next to *talking*.

Use the TLT Triangle to explain communication:

1. We use our brain to think. (Think about what the other person is saying, think about what we want to say when it's our turn.)

2. We use our ears to listen. (Listen to what people are saying.)

3. We use our mouth to talk. (Talk when it's our turn.)

Ask the child to draw two people who are communicating with each other inside the triangle. Ask the following questions:

1. What is each person thinking about before they talk?

2. Who is talking?

3. Who is listening?

4. What is the talker doing?

5. What is the listener doing?

TLT Triangle: THINKING, LISTENING, TALKING

Listening

Thinking   Talking

How to be a good listener

Talking seems to come naturally to most of us. More often than not, children who are talkative need a better understanding of what it means to listen well. Share the following tips, taking time to model each for the child:

- Your ears are listening to the person talking.
- Your eyes are looking straight ahead at the person talking, making eye contact if possible.
- Your brain is thinking about what the person is talking about.
- Your mind is focused on understanding what the other person is saying.
- Your mouth is closed.
- Your tongue is relaxed.
- Your arms are by your sides and on your own body.
- Your body is relaxed.
- You wait for the person to stop talking before you talk.
- You think about what to say before you say it.

Tips for parents

- Show your child you want to listen to him. Set aside some one-on-one time with the child daily and give focused attention. You are teaching him how to communicate and listen to others. If possible, try planning 15 to 30 minutes of talk time at the same time daily. Go to a quiet place. Turn off technology. Make direct eye contact and show your interest with facial expressions. Listen and repeat what he is saying without interrupting. Ask questions about his story to better understand and show you were paying attention. Encourage fast talkers to slow down.
- Set limits when you need quiet time. For example, you could say, "Between 5:30 and 6:00, I would like my own quiet time. You can draw, play, listen to music in another room, or pick your own activity."

- Praise the child when she is not interrupting. "I liked how you did not interrupt me when I was talking on the phone."
- If the child has siblings, try using a timer to make sure everyone has a turn telling their story.

What to avoid

- Avoid labeling the talkative child as a chatterbox or the dramatic kid in the family.
- Avoid sighing and rolling your eyes when the talkative child rambles on and on.
- Avoid comments like "You never stop talking" and "Don't you ever get tired of talking?"

Helping talkative children learn and practice listening skills at home

- Simon Says is a fun way to teach listening skills. Children learn to pay attention to when you say "Simon Says" and when you don't.
- Make up a story and ask the child to draw the scenes you describe. Use lots of details in the story so the child will pay attention, knowing she will have to re-create the scene later.
- Take a walk outside and invite the child to listen carefully and identify the sounds he hears. Discuss what sounds he might miss due to talking.

Parents can communicate with school staff about the talkative child

- Communicate with your child's teacher(s) before school starts and ask how the teacher manages talkative children. List your child's strengths and talents. Discuss solutions. Attend school conferences to stay updated. Stay informed on your child's progress.

Tips for educators

- Put a positive spin on the energy of a talkative youngster. For example, you could say, "I like listening to your fun facts and stories, but I also like it when you listen to my stories."
- Praise the child when she is not interrupting. "I liked how you did not interrupt me when I was talking to another student."
- For children who like to talk during announcements or movies, give them index cards and tell them to write things down to share when the program is over.

Helping talkative children in the school classroom

- Clearly spell out to the entire class the rules with regard to talking (raising hands and so on). Take time to practice the rules and enforce them uniformly and consistently.
- Collaborate with a talkative child's parents, ask how they manage the talkativeness at home, and share strategies so the approach is consistent between school and home.

About the Author

Melissa Martin, Ph.D., is a clinical child therapist with experience as a play therapist, adjunct professor, workshop leader and trainer, and behavioral health consultant. Her specializations include mental health trauma treatment, EMDR (Eye Movement Desensitization and Reprocessing), and expressive therapies. A self-syndicated newspaper columnist, she writes on children's mental health issues and parenting. Melissa lives in Ohio.

About the Illustrator

Charles Lehman enjoys illustrating children's stories. He lives and works out of his studio in Orlando, Florida, with his wife and four children. He remembers the countless times his parents and friends tried to help him learn to tame his own tongue, which sometimes got him into trouble like Tessie.

Other Great Books from Free Spirit

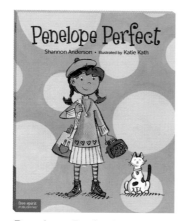

Penelope Perfect
A Tale of Perfectionism Gone Wild
by Shannon Anderson, illustrated by Katie Kath
48 pp., color illust., PB and HC, 8" x 10".
Ages 5–9.

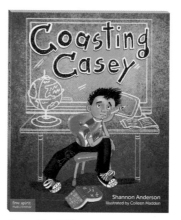

Coasting Casey
A Tale of Busting Boredom in School
by Shannon Anderson, illustrated by Colleen Madden
48 pp., color illust., PB and HC, 8" x 10".
Ages 5–9.

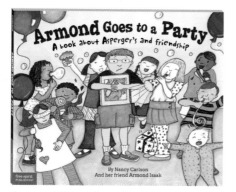

Armond Goes to a Party
A book about Asperger's and friendship
by Nancy Carlson and her friend Armond Isaak
32 pp., color illust., PB and HC, 11¼" x 9¼". Ages 5–9.

This Morning Sam Went to Mars
A book about paying attention
by Nancy Carlson
32 pp., color illust., PB and HC, 11¼" x 9¼". Ages 5–9.

Interested in purchasing multiple quantities and receiving volume discounts?
Contact edsales@freespirit.com or call 1.800.735.7323 and ask for Education Sales.

Many Free Spirit authors are available for speaking engagements, workshops, and keynotes.
Contact speakers@freespirit.com or call 1.800.735.7323.

For pricing information, to place an order, or to request a free catalog, contact:

Free Spirit Publishing Inc.
6325 Sandburg Road • Suite 100 • Minneapolis, MN 55427-3674
toll-free 800.735.7323 • local 612.338.2068 • fax 612.337.5050
help4kids@freespirit.com • www.freespirit.com